For my big bro Bij, with love

PUFFIN BOOKS

UK | USA | Canada | Ireland | Australia
India | New Zealand | South Africa

Puffin Books is part of the Penguin Random House group of companies
whose addresses can be found at global.penguinrandomhouse.com.

www.penguin.co.uk   www.puffin.co.uk   www.ladybird.co.uk

Penguin
Random House
UK

First published 2022

001

Text and illustrations copyright © Jion Sheibani, 2022

The moral right of the author/illustrator has been asserted

Text design by Kim Musselle
Printed and bound in China by RR Donnelley Asia Printing Solutions

The authorized representative in the EEA is Penguin Random House Ireland,
Morrison Chambers, 32 Nassau Street, Dublin D02 YH68

A CIP catalogue record for this book is available from the British Library

ISBN: 978–0–241–57220–7

All correspondence to:
Puffin Books
Penguin Random House Children's
One Embassy Gardens, 8 Viaduct Gardens
London, SW11 7BW

*The publishers would like to thank Possibility People for their
helpful insights into the sensitivity aspects of the text.*

THE WORRIES

SHARA AND THE REALLY BIG SLEEPOVER

PUFFIN

Shara and Keita were having dinner at their **favourite** pizza restaurant with their mum.

'Order anything you like!' Mum said.
'Today's a special day!'

Shara was excited about ordering whatever she liked, but she did not think there was anything special about today. Why were they **celebrating** Mum going on holiday by herself, **WITHOUT HER AND KEITA**, while they had to go to stay at their grandad's?!

OK, she loved Baba. A lot! But it was the first time they'd ever stayed at his new flat. He used to live a long way away but had moved nearer to be closer to them all. Mum kept telling Shara and Keita that it would be like one giant fun sleepover, but that didn't reassure Shara. The last sleepover she'd been to, her mum had had to come and pick her up early. It was SO embarrassing.

But Shara didn't want to think about that now.

For a whole hour and eight minutes, Shara
and Keita (nearly) forgot about Mum's trip.
Instead, they made themselves busy arguing
about . . .

whose colouring page was more **amazing** ...

whose pizza was **fatter** ...

and whose idea it was to put their drinking
straws in their noses and snort bubbles.

Oh, AND enjoying their pizza too, of
course! It was **THE BEST PIZZA EVER**.
Plus the ice-cream machine was **EAT AS
MUCH AS YOU LIKE** (*even* the
toppings!).

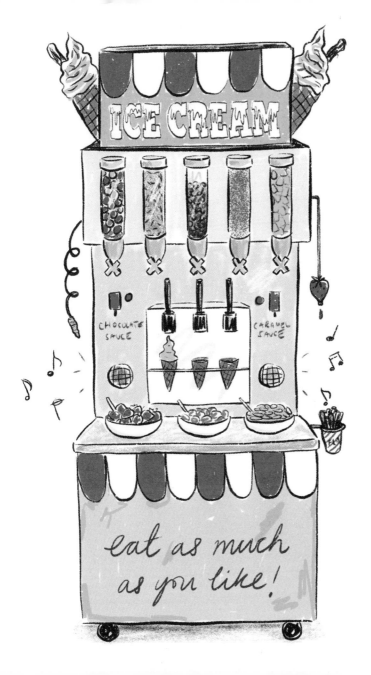

ICE CREAM

CHOCOLATE
SAUCE

CARAMEL
SAUCE

eat as much
as you like!

But when they got back to the car, Shara started to feel a bit different. She missed the noise and light of the restaurant. The sky was darker now, and their empty house would also be dark when they got home.

She started to think about Mum going away again … but then immediately pushed the thought to the back of her head. She was the big sister – she would need to look after Keita.

Shara turned round to look at Keita. Somehow he was wrestling with his seat belt **AND** whingeing **AND** picking his nose, all at the same time!

'Here, I'll do it,' Shara said, rolling her eyes.

'**NO, I CAN DO IT**!' Keita snapped.

'O-kaaaaayyyyy,' Shara said, sighing.

'Are you all right, sweetheart?' Mum asked her, as they drove towards home. 'You look . . . *worried.*'

Shara looked at Mum's frowning face and gave her a big fake smile. She didn't want her to worry too. 'Yep!' she said breezily. 'I'm fine.'

'Oh, good,' Mum said, relieved. 'Are you excited about staying with Baba tomorrow?

He can't wait to see you!'

The thought of her grandad and his cosy new flat did perk Shara up a bit. But before she could answer, Keita started moaning again.

'I don't want you to **GOOOO, MUUUUUUM!**'

'I know, Keita,' Mum said soothingly. 'But mums need holidays too. The whole netball team are going. Besides, you're going to have a **BRILLIANT** time with Baba. He's got lots of fun things planned.'

'It's NOT going to be *brilliant*,' Keita said moodily, taking out his pot of slime to play with. He started making loud, farting noises with it.

PARP!

PARP!

PARP!

Keita was so busy making these noises and giggling and making Mum and Shara giggle too that he didn't notice that the slime was looking

EVER

SO

SLIGHTLY

DIFFERENT...

Chapter 2

When they got home, Shara put ALL the lights in the house on so that it was nice and bright and welcoming.

'All right, Shara, it's not a Christmas lights display!' Mum said, chuckling, as she came up behind her on the stairlift.

But Shara wasn't listening. She was already in her bedroom, staring at the bag she was supposed to be taking to Baba's. But instead of packing, she sat down at her desk and took out her homework.

Whenever she started feeling worried, Shara liked to **Get On With Other Things**.

She'd actually already finished her homework, but Shara wanted to make sure the letters were

PERFECT and that everything was underlined **BEAUTIFULLY**.

She was rubbing out a letter for the **MILLIONTH** time when something *moved* inside her pencil case.

Eek! What was that?!

A small, six-fingered hand was now pulling at the zip. Suddenly, a familiar little head with incredibly neat hair and **GIGANTIC** glasses popped out.

6 fingers (handy on the piano)

bow-tie for looking dapper at all times - even in the bath

4 arms for doing a million things at once

braces, like the good old days!

tail for whacking anyone who does not OBEY

briefcase full of nice stationery

super clean + ironed socks

Reece Sponsible

'HIII, SHARA!' he sang.
           'IT'S ONLY MEEEEEE!'

'**Oh noooo**,' moaned Shara. It was

her Worry, Reece Sponsable. He'd been

appearing on and off for the past three

YEARS now. Shara still remembered that

dreaded day at the

zoo when Reece

had first appeared.

Let's not forget, I did ALSO save your delightful brother from getting trampled by a zebra!

'Eugh, I wish you wouldn't DO that!' Shara cried.

'Do what?'

'Read my mind like that. You should really ask my permission first.'

'Permission?! Oh, *please*. I came **OUT** of your mind. I know that place better than **YOU** do. I don't need *permission*!'

Reece jumped out of the pencil case and strutted towards Shara. He picked up the paper Shara was writing on and looked at it disapprovingly.

'DON'T tell me this is your homework?!'

'Why? What's wrong with it?' Shara asked, looking terribly hurt.

'Ha! What's **RIGHT** with it, you mean?
First of all, you've committed the absolute
WORST homework crime of all time.'

'Oh yeah, and what's *that* then?'

'You've rubbed out SO many times, you
can see…' Reece gulped. '**THE MARKS
UNDERNEATH!**' He rummaged around
in his briefcase and plucked out a gleaming
white eraser. He held it out to Shara like
treasure. 'Now THIS is an eraser! You'll
see. It'll make it all **PURRRRFECT!**'
He clawed the air like a very strange cat.

'Eugh, I wish you'd just… *go* please, Reece.'
Shara sighed, taking the eraser reluctantly.
She was relieved – but also annoyed – to see

that the eraser had worked beautifully.

'I told –' Reece began.

'Do NOT say *I told you so!*' Shara
snapped.

'OK, OK!' Reece sighed dramatically. He
turned his attention to Shara's bedroom and
began to inspect it with his **GOOGLY** eyes.
He opened his mouth to speak again when
suddenly Shara had a brainwave.

'Oh, Reece, I forgot to tell you,' she
said quickly. 'I've got some **SHINY** new
stationery!'

Reece's tiny ears pricked up. 'Oh, you
know how much I LOVE new stationery,'
he said, clapping all four hands together and

swishing his spiky tail. 'Remember that
beautiful little shop in France –'

'Er, actually I'd rather not,' Shara interrupted. (It had been a *very* traumatic holiday.) She opened her stationery drawer and showed Reece some special new glitter pens, tiny Post-it Notes, a box of pretty paper clips and a set of **FIZZY-DRINK-FLAVOUR CRAYONS**. Mum had bought them for her birthday, and Shara had been saving them for a special occasion. She hadn't imagined this would be the special occasion, but she REALLY wanted her Worry to go away. 'Look, here you go, Reece! It's ALL yours.'

Reece greedily hurried towards the drawer, and once he was inside, Shara shoved it SHUT. It was surprising how easily Worries could be distracted sometimes.

'Ooh, it's a bit **DARK!**' she heard Reece shout. 'Hang on, I've got a torch in here somewhere . . .' Shara heard loud clattering as Reece emptied the contents of his briefcase. 'Found it!' he eventually called. 'Oh, that's *much* better. What **GORGEOUS** stationery! It's like Ali Baba's cave in here.'

Phew, thought Shara, getting back to her homework. *THAT should keep him busy for a while . . .*

Chapter 3

'Oh my goodness,' Mum gasped an hour later, after she'd finished packing for her holiday. 'You're STILL not in bed, Keita?! Your sister's already fast asleep, you know!'

Keita was stretching the **GLOOPY SLIME** between his fingers.

He looked up at Mum. **'SORRYYYY.'**

'And look at the state of your room!'

'I was finding toys to take to Baba's . . .'

Mum looked at the enormous suitcase that Keita had somehow dragged down from the cupboard. It was now FULL of his toys.

'Right,' Mum said, taking a breath. 'Well, I'm not sure that's the world's most practical packing, Keita . . . but let's concentrate on getting into bed now. We'll sort this out in the morning.'

'Can I still have a story?' Keita asked, snuggling under his quilt. He was still clutching his slime and trying to shove it back into the pot.

'Just the one,' Mum said, smiling.

'And sing our song?'

'Just the once!' Mum propped her crutch beside his bed and lay down next to him.

'Yeeaaaaah!' Keita squealed, wriggling with excitement and making farting noises with his slime again.

PARP!

PARP!

PARP!

'Erm, you're going to have to put that slime away, Keita,' Mum said firmly.

'But I can't get the lid on!' he whined. 'It's **GROWN!**'

'Don't be silly,' Mum said. 'Here, I'll do it.'

Mum squished and squashed and pushed and pounded but she couldn't get the slime back in the pot either!

'**EUGH!**' she groaned. 'I give up! Let's just put it down here.' And she placed the pot of slime on the floor.

'OK, ready?' Mum said, clicking her fingers rhythmically. Keita grinned and joined in too. Then they sang:

Bedtime Boogie boogie boogie boogie boogie!

Bedtime boogie! (click click click)

Won't you woogie woogie

woogie woogie woogie?

Woogie with me? (click click click)

We've brushed our teeth and been to the loo.

(Don't tell me if it's a wee or a poo.)

Bedtime boogie woogie boogie woogie woo.

Ooh ooh oooooooooooooh!(jazz hands)

'**AGAIN!**' Keita giggled.

'No, it's story time now!' Mum said.

'It's getting late.'

Keita groaned and pulled out a huge

stack of his favourite bedtime stories from

under the bed. 'I can't **CHOOSE!** I want ALL of them,' he whined.

'Let's do this one,' Mum suggested, taking the one that was on top of the pile. 'This was always your favourite, even when you were a baby.'

She started to read the book and Keita helped her do the funny voices and sounds. It was a very noisy story! Keita loved it.

On the last pages, though, the words and pictures became quieter and softer – just right for getting ready to go to sleep.

Keita didn't want it to end. '**AGAIN!**' he said as soon as Mum read the last page.

'No, my love. It's time to go to sleep now.' Mum whispered. 'Have you been to the toilet?'

Keita nodded.

'Are you sure?' Mum insisted. Sometimes Keita wet the bed at night, especially when he was worried. Mum had bought him some pull-up pants but he didn't always feel like wearing them.

'**YES!**' he said irritably. He was very embarrassed about the bed-wetting and did **NOT** like anyone talking about it.

'OK, OK,' Mum said gently. 'Well, close your eyes then, love.'

'But . . . it's too *dark* behind my eyes!' Keita moaned.

As soon as he said it, something suddenly sprang on to Keita's side of the bed. It looked like Keita's slime! Except now it had eyes and a mouth!

Keita screamed. 'AAAAAAAAGH!'

'What's the matter?!' Mum cried.

'Er, nothing,' Keita said, grabbing the slime before she could see. 'I just thought there was a . . . spider . . . but it's gone.'

'OK, love.'

Keita shoved the slime

under his pillow, right where his head lay.
Only . . . now he could hear it talking!

'Please don't be afraid of me,' the slime
was saying, in a wobbly, jelly-like voice.
'I'm just your Worry – Scared. I would say

Wonky SCARED smile

3 eyes to look out for DANGER

WAAH

slime

handy pot for hiding in

SCARED

"pleased" to meet you
but that wouldn't be
very honest of me.
I'm actually pretty . . .

SCARED!'

Mum sat up, frowning.
'What was that noise?'
'Oh, nothing!' Keita
said, giving Mum his best
innocent look. 'I was just . . . talking to myself.'

'OK . . .' she said suspiciously.

'Get her to read the story one more time!' the slime whispered.

'No!' whispered Keita out of the side of his mouth.

Mum looked at him strangely. 'Right... I think you must be tired now, Keita, so let's say goodnight.' She gave him a big CUDDLE. 'And don't look so worried! I'm only going to be away for two sleeps. Besides, you know you'll have a lovely time with Baba. Sweet dreams, darling.'

Mum put Keita's night lights on, blew him a final kiss and left the door wide open, just how he liked it.

As his head sank into his pillow, Keita tried really hard not to listen to his Worry squirming around under his pillow or think about wetting the bed. Instead, he thought about Baba and all the yummy treats he would have in his fridge. His eyelids got heavier and heavier, and soon Keita drifted off to sleep, dreaming mostly of food . . .

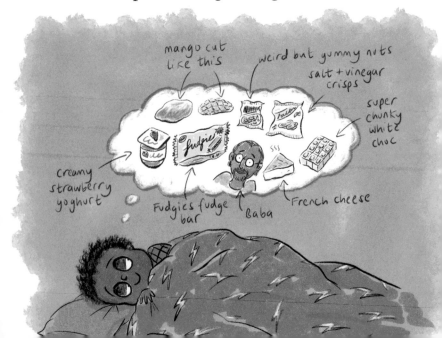

Chapter 4

The next morning, Mum, Shara and Keita were woken by a different kind of alarm clock. It was the loud, maddening **BEEP BEEP BEEP** of the smoke alarm going off. By the time they heard it, they could also smell burnt toast wafting through the house. At first Mum thought it must be Shara, and

Shara thought it must be Keita, and Keita thought it must be . . . his tortoise (he did have a pretty big imagination).

But when Shara and Keita padded downstairs and opened the kitchen door, Shara immediately saw who it was. There was Reece Sponsable, perched inside the fridge, loading a ridiculous number of breakfast things on to a tray. He had grown since last night but was still far too small to carry it, even with his four arms and tail.

'**Woah, cooool!**' Keita gasped. 'Are you . . . a dinosaur?!'

'**HELLO!**' he cried. 'Don't mind us. Just hop
back into bed, why don't you?! We'll bring
this upstairs to you.'

'Hang on – we?! Who's we?' Shara said
suspiciously. She peered into the fridge, and
was amazed to find Scared frantically passing
things to Reece.

'Hiiiii!' he said weakly.

'That's Scared,' Keita said to Shara, a bit
embarrassed. 'I thought he was still under my
pillow . . .'

'And I thought Reece Sponsable was still
in my stationery drawer . . .' Shara sighed. Her
Worry was bad enough, but seeing that Keita
had one too only made her even more anxious.

'Everything all right?' Mum called from the top of the stairlift.

'Er, **YES ... YES, FINE!**' Shara shouted. '**JUST ME ... BURNING TOAST. SILLY ME!**' She turned to the Worries. 'Right, just leave everything on the table and hide! Mum's on her way down!'

'Whatever I'm in trouble for, HE made me do it,' Scared said, pointing to Reece. Then he bounced towards an open pot of strawberry jam and jumped right into it.

'Not **THERE!**' Keita yelped, pulling him right out again. 'That's Mum's favourite!' He opened the cherry jam instead. 'Here, she hates this one. She'll never find you in there!'

Shara pulled Scared straight out again.

'Eugh, Keitaaaa! He's even stickier now!
Plus I don't want bits of him in our food!
GROSS!' She pushed Scared into a packet

of weird cereal that had
been in the cupboard
for **YEARS**.

Shara looked around
the kitchen for Reece,
but she couldn't find
him. He was VERY
good at hiding, which

was fortunate because, right then, Mum
came into the room.

'**HI,** Mum. **BYE**, Mum. I'm going to get dressed!' Shara shouted, trying to sound as chilled-out as possible but failing massively. Before running out of the kitchen, she whispered in her brother's ear, 'Keep that cereal packet shut, OK? No matter what!'

Keita, whose mouth was full of yoghurt and toast and blueberries **AND** cornflakes, pretended he'd heard and nodded obediently (although actually he was reading the cornflakes box very intently, and hadn't really heard what she'd said).

When Shara went upstairs to the bathroom, she was surprised to see the door was shut. And yet Mum and Keita were definitely still downstairs. *Perhaps it was just the wind*, she thought. She paused in front of the door.

'Hello?! Is there . . . someone in there . . .?'

Silence.

'Nooooooo!' a voice suddenly wailed.

'Not someone! I'm a **NO ONE**. BOOHooooooo HOOooooooo!'

Shara turned the handle, opened the door and found a skinny, peculiar thing standing in the bath, wearing snorkelling gear. He was waist-deep in water, with his knees to his chest, but Shara soon realized that the water was in fact all the **tears** running down his cheeks!

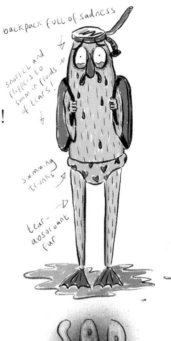

backpack full of sadness

snorkel and flippers to swim in floods of tears!

swimming trunks

tear-absorbant fur

SAD

The Worry looked up at Shara. 'Where's Keita?'

'He's downstairs. But who are you?'

'I need to find him!' he moaned, standing up. 'I want to get out of the bath. Get me out now!'

'No, don't go bothering him, please. We're going to be late for school!'

Right then, Keita came bounding into the bathroom to brush his teeth.

'There you are!' The creature sobbed, jumping into Keita's arms.

'Er, do I know you?' Keita said, trying to push it away.

'Of course you do! I'm **SAD!**' He turned to Shara. 'You see, **I TOLD** you I was a **NO ONE.** Not even **HE** recognizes me – and I'm **HIS** Worry!'

Shara noticed that Sad's wet fur was soaking Keita's uniform. She quickly dried him with a towel and was about to use the hairdryer when she heard a noise coming from Mum's bedroom.

THUMP THUMP
THUMP
CLANG!

Shara marched across the landing towards the noise but was stopped in her tracks by a pair of **knickers** flying through the air (thankfully, clean). More things followed: clothes, shoes, books, toiletries . . . and with each flying object came a loud grunting sound.

'UGG! OOG! HUMPF! GRR!'

As Shara crept closer, though, it suddenly stopped.

'Come out, come out, whatever you are!' Shara called. 'I'm not going to hurt you. Promise.'

'I don't *trust* promises!' a gruff voice came back.

'Well, you can trust *this* promise,' Shara said, tiptoeing closer. She could see something twitching under a pile of clothes next to Mum's suitcase. She quickly whipped off Mum's flowery dress, but the thing darted away before

Shara could catch it. All she saw was a flash of orange. Then it was gone. She searched under all the other clothes and in all the suitcase pockets . . . but there was no sign of it.

'**Eugh, fine**,' Shara said reluctantly, looking at the mess around her. She started folding Mum's things and putting them back into the suitcase.

'Everything all right, sweetheart?' Mum called up the stairs.

'**Yeah, fine!**' Shara shouted back.

  She zipped Mum's suitcase shut, put the lock on it just to be sure,

and carried it downstairs with hers and Keita's going-away bags.

'What was that noise?' Mum frowned when Shara sat back down for breakfast.

'Oh . . . just some books . . . falling.'

Shara didn't like lying but she also didn't like being late for school. Besides, it was only half a lie. Books had fallen. She just didn't say how!

Chapter 5

When they got to the school gates, Shara bent down and gave Mum a quick kiss goodbye.

'Don't I get a proper hug?!' Mum said.

Shara turned round and let herself be hugged. **'CHOP. CHOP!'** she heard Reece hiss from inside her pocket. 'No time for all that nonsense – you're going to be **LATE!**'

Keita jumped on to Mum's lap and wrapped his arms round her. 'Have a brilliant holiday, Mum!'

Suddenly the bell rang and Mr Yeung, the head teacher, started closing the gate.

'I will, darling. Off you go now!' Mum said, letting go of Keita and waving them both goodbye.

As soon as Mum left, Shara saw a flash of orange jump

out of Keita's pocket and run towards the gate. Shara realized this must be the Worry that had been throwing things out of Mum's suitcase earlier. How had it got here?

'You **CAN'T GOOOO!**' the creature yelled, trying to climb the railings with its three little legs.

Reece ran towards it and tried to pull it off by the scruff of its neck.

'**HEY!** Get your hands off me!' it cried. The two of them started scrapping.

Shara ran over. 'Stop it!' she shouted. '**EVERYONE** is looking!'

Just then, a tiny little mouse-like thing with lots of eyes and a very strange nose appeared.

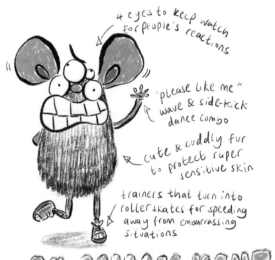

4 eyes to keep watch for people's reactions

"please like me" wave & side-kick dance combo

cute & cuddly fur to protect super sensitive skin

trainers that turn into rollerskates for speeding away from embarrassing situations

EM BARRASS-MENT

'YES, PLEASE STOP!'

it squeaked.

'PLEASE PLEASE PLEASE?!'

'Who are you?' Shara yelped. 'Not **ANOTHER** Worry!?'

'Er, I'm afraid so . . . **I'm Em. Em Barrass-Ment**. Enchanted to meet you! And sorry . . . for appearing like this!'

'Em Barrass-Ment,' Shara said slowly. 'Embarrassment? Seriously?! That's all I need!' She sighed. She picked up the other

Worry, who was trying to wrestle Reece. 'So, who on EARTH are you?'

'What's it to you?' the spiky-haired creature said, hands on hips. 'I'm not **YOUR** Worry.'

'Well, you might as well be. You're picking fights with mine! Plus, I don't see Keita stopping you from making a scene.'

'OK then, clever clogs. I'm Badbye, if you really need to know. And my pronoun is "they", all right?'

'OK. But . . . Badbye?'

'Yeah, cos there's no such thing as goodbye. Get it? **BAD**bye. Now THAT'S clever!'

'Right, well, I'm definitely leaving you with Keita. I've got to get to class now. Come on, Em . . . **GOOD**bye!' Shara started to walk away, fast, with Em scampering after her.

'You're not going anywhere!' Badbye said, leaping on to Shara's shoe. The Worry quickly tied Shara's laces together (without actually knowing how to do it properly).

Shara lifted one foot and it came undone immediately. 'Nice try, Badbye.'

Suddenly Badbye snatched Scared out of Reece Sponsable's arms. They opened the lid of Scared's pot and stretched Scared between their fingers.

'No one leaves, otherwise the Worry **GETS IT!**'

There was a loud gasp from Sad. Scared started whimpering.

'PUT HIM DOWN!' Reece shouted, wielding the first thing he could find in his briefcase: a very brown banana. Shara noticed that Reece was also

53

wearing a police hat from goodness knows where. Surely that couldn't fit in a **BRIEFCASE?**

'Oh dear, oh dear!' Em squealed, running round them in circles.

'Right,' Shara said, pulling Scared out of Badbye's hands. 'I think that's enough drama for one morning.' She pushed Scared back into his pot.

'Good morning! Everything all right here?' Mr Yeung said merrily.

'Good morning, Mr Yeung!' Shara beamed while Badbye yanked her leg. 'Everything's absolutely fine, thank you!'

Reece pulled Badbye off Shara

actual hair gel = COOL!

Mr Yeung

New Headmaster

Super NICE

everyone agrees he is 20 or 21 MAX

and shoved them into Shara's bag. Em wiped her sweaty brow and clapped her hands enthusiastically.

'Oh, bravo, Reece! Thank you! That's one less thing to be embarrassed about, ha ha!'

Mr Yeung looked at Keita and

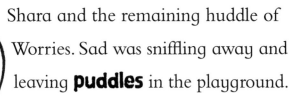

Shara and the remaining huddle of Worries. Sad was sniffling away and leaving **puddles** in the playground. Scared was bouncing out of his pot again. Em Barrass-Ment was apologizing non-stop.

And Reece, of course, was just trying to shoo everyone along to class.

'There there, you'll be fine!!' Mr Yeung smiled, taking Sad's hand, while Keita took the other. Shara picked up Em and Reece and put them in the side pocket of her rucksack.

'Oh, phew!' Em sighed. 'At last, a nice snug place to **HIDE**!'

'Hey, put me down!' Reece yelped. 'What on earth do you think you're doing?!'

'Well, I can't just walk in with my Worries – everyone will see!' Shara cried.

'Oh, that's **REALLY NICE**,' Reece said sarcastically.

'She does have a jolly good point!'
Em chipped in. 'It would be absolutely
AWFUL.'

'Hey – what about **ME?!**' Scared
trembled, slithering up her leg. 'You gotta
take **ME!**'

'You're not my Worry!' Shara hissed as
they got to Keita's classroom. 'Hey, Keita,
take him off me, will you? I've already got
Badbye in here.'

Keita looked at her with his big,
worried eyes. Sad was still sobbing away.
'But I can't take **BOTH** of them! What will
my friends say?'

Shara spotted her own friends further

down the corridor. What would HER friends say if they saw this weird **slimy creature** stuck to her?!

'OK,' she said, giving in and shoving Scared into her bag. 'Just this once. But I'm giving him back to you at break time.'

'Thanks, Shara,' Keita said, hugging her round the waist. Then with Sad stuffed under his jumper, he scuttled into his classroom.

Chapter 6

When she got to class, Shara found it impossible to concentrate because of Scared's non-stop whimpering. **EVERYTHING** made him jump: the computer turning on, Mr Chatterjee calling the register, a chair leg scraping the floor ... Song Time was unbearable. To make things worse, every time Scared had a meltdown, Reece would pop up to **WHACK** him over the head and shove him back into his pot. Then Badbye would get angry with Scared and Reece for waking them up from their nap (of which there were many).

Meanwhile, Em Barrass-Ment tried many desperate and slightly rubbish attempts to distract

I am trying to SLEEP!

everyone
from what
was going on.

'Hey, cut it out,
you lot!' Shara whispered.

'Are you all right, Shara?' Mr Chatterjee
asked, seeing her crouch under the desk
yet again.

'Yes, it's just my . . . well, not both mine . . .
I can't really explain . . . I just . . . dropped my
pencil, that's all! Oh, look, here it is!'

'Riiiight. OK,' Mr Chatterjee said, frowning.
'Let's focus on these sums, shall we?'

'Ooh, I don't like SUMS!' Scared
whispered.

'No one **CARES** if you like them or
not,' Reece hissed. 'They're simply necessary.
Now, stop distracting Shara and SHUSH!'

'Yes, stop distracting Shara and SHUSH!'
Em squeaked.

'I **JUST** said that,' Reece snapped.

'Sorry!' Em whispered.

Reece rolled his eyes. 'And **STOP** saying

$10 \times 11 = 110$

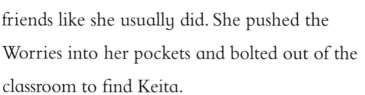

SORRY!'

'Sor–OK,' Em said, nodding obediently.

Shara was practically counting the seconds until break time. As soon as the bell rang, she didn't wait for her friends like she usually did. She pushed the Worries into her pockets and bolted out of the classroom to find Keita.

This wasn't difficult – she quickly realized she could hear him crying from the other side of the playground.

Shara hurried over to him, and he flung his arms round her. As she hugged him back, she

$\sqrt{6}$

180

$4 + 9 = 23$

$?^2 = ?$

spotted Sad behind Keita. As if he wasn't already embarrassing enough, he was now wearing a rubber ring and armbands. Shara wondered if this was one of the reasons Keita was crying. It was drawing quite a lot of attention to him . . .

'So, what's up, squirt?' she asked Keita.

'I . . . I . . . I have a . . .

HUGE

SPELLING TEST!'

he blubbered.

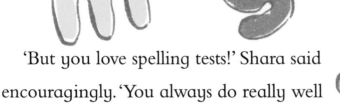

'But you love spelling tests!' Shara said encouragingly. 'You always do really well in them.'

'I KNOW! EXACTLY! But it's **TOMORROW**, and Mum won't be here to help me practise so I'm going to do **REALLY BADLY!**' He burst into tears again.

'Well, I can help you!' Shara said, squeezing his shoulders. 'Or Baba.'

'It's not **THE SAME!**' Keita cried.

Just then Keita's friends came over.

'You OK?' they asked.

'Do you want to play?'

'I know, let's play with your slime instead!'

Uh-oh.

The pot containing Scared had been in Shara's pocket, but it must have rolled on to the floor when she hugged Keita. Of course, it did look like a pot of slime – but before Shara could say anything, one of Keita's friends, Harry, picked it up and peeled the lid off. He didn't notice Scared's *terrified* eyes staring back at him.

'Here, this will cheer you up, Keita. I'll show you a really cool slime trick!'

'Hey!' Keita shouted in a panic. 'Give that back!'

'It's just one quick trick!' Harry said,

yanking Scared out of the pot and stretching him as far as possible. Scared looked petrified now.

'Give it back, please, Harry,' Shara said, holding out her hand.

But Harry wasn't listening. 'Look, if you just twist it . . . and throw it . . . then spin it like this . . . Ta-da! How cool is that?!'

Sad landed in Harry's palm with a **SPLAT** – squished, cross-eyed and breathless. Keita started crying again.

Harry rolled his eyes. '**OK, OK!** I was just trying to cheer you up!'

Just then, Shara's friends Sohal and Jaz came over.

'Hey, everything OK?' asked Jaz. 'What's the matter?'

'Oh, nothing,' Shara said. 'It's just Keita being a bit dramatic. Mum's gone away for a couple of nights and he's really upset about it.'

'I'm **NOT** being dramatic,' Keita cried. He folded his arms and turned his back to his sister.

'You know, there's a really cool room at school now where you can go and chat about your worries,' Sohal said to Keita, eyeing the chaos around them. 'The lady who runs it is really nice too.'

'Yeah, she gives you juice and stickers!'

Jaz added kindly.

Keita's eyes brightened. 'Can I go there now?' he asked.

'Yeah, we'll take you!'

Sohal and Jaz led the way while Shara, Keita and the Worries trundled behind them. They eventually arrived at the room, which was right next to the library.

It had a colourful sign saying:

The door was ajar, and they could see that there were lots of bright cushions on the floor and fun posters on the walls. They said things like:

A PROBLEM SHARED IS A PROBLEM HALVED

A smiley lady came to the door and introduced herself as Abby.

Hi. I'm Keita, and this is my big sister, Shara. Oh, and these are my Worries: **SAD** and **SCARED**.

Hi, Keita. Hi, Shara! And hello, **SAD** and **SCARED**.

Abby said.

Would you all like to come in for a chat?

71

Keita nodded and gave a shy smile.

Sad nodded too. 'I would really really
LOVE that,' he said, laughing *and* crying
at the same time.

'Ooh, I'm not so suuuuure,' Scared
whispered.

Abby looked at Shara. 'Would you like to
join us too?'

Shara thought about it for a second. She
did quite want to go in, but then she felt
something prodding her in the back. It was
Reece Sponsable's **SHARP** little finger.

'You don't need that nonsense,' Reece
murmured. 'You're perfectly capable of
managing by yourself. Besides, your friends

are waiting for you!'

'Yeah, and it's **WAY** too embarrassing!' Em whispered. 'That lady seems nice and everything, but she is a **COMPLETE** stranger! You don't want to tell her your WORRIES!'

Shara turned back to look at Sohal and Jaz. She did want to have some break time with them, at least.

She shook her head at Abby. 'Ah, no, thanks. I'm fine! BYE!'

Then she ran back outside to play with her friends.

Although Reece Sponsable had other ideas . . .

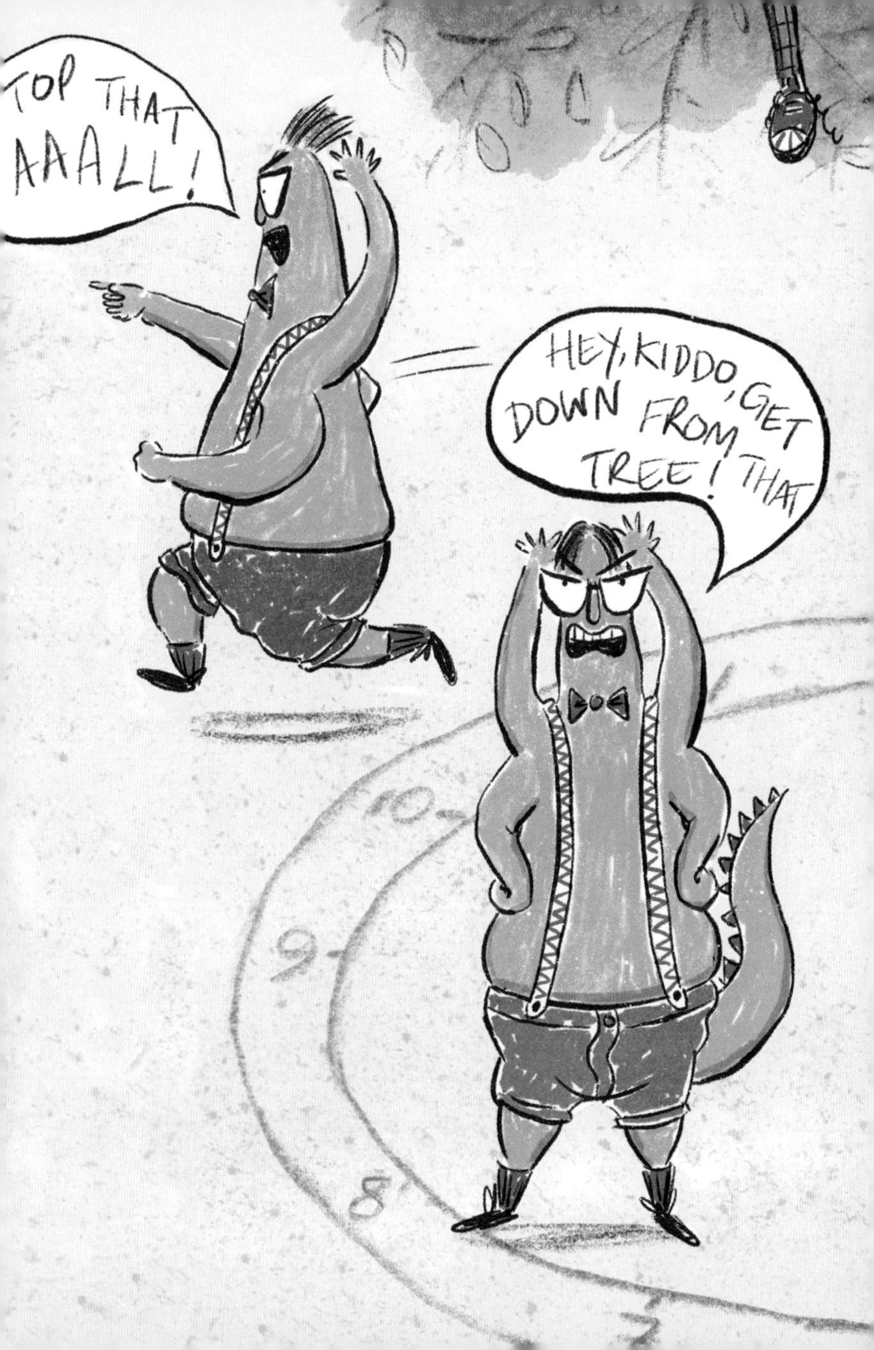
TOP THAT AAALL!
HEY, KIDDO, GET DOWN FROM TREE! THAT

Chapter 7

After bugging Shara **ALL** day, Reece finally calmed down right before home time, when Mr Chatterjee read them a brilliant story. Reece stayed calm even after the bell rang and Shara ran to meet her grandad at the school gates.

But Em Barrass-Ment did not.

'Hello, my beautiful lion!' Baba said, stretching his arms out to hug her. Baba had called Shara 'beautiful lion' since she was a baby because of her lovely big mane of hair. Usually she liked it, but now it was really annoying – **especially** right in front of the school gates with **everybody** looking.

'Hi, Baba.' Shara smiled awkwardly, walking into his hug.

Em quickly tugged at Shara's jumper and pulled her back. 'That was WAY too long a hug!' she squeaked. 'Especially a public hug!

Keep it **COOL!**'

'Says the un-coolest Worry ever,'
Shara mumbled, rolling her eyes.

Keita came sprinting up behind
them. '**BABA!**' he screamed,
jumping into his arms. Baba started
to tickle him, and he fell about giggling.

'Who's ready for . . .

MILKSHAKES?!'
Baba boomed.

'**ME ME ME!**'
Keita yelled.

Shara
loved Baba's
milkshakes,

because he made them
himself with ice cream and
actual fruit and usually
sang a silly song while he
did it.

'Guess what else?' Baba
said, taking them by the hand
and dancing down the street.
'I've made your favourite dinner tonight!'

'Your special rice?' Keita said.

'YEAH!'

'And homemade bread?'

'YEAH!'

'And that delicious veggie stew?'

'YEAH YEAH YEAH!'

'WAHOOOOO!'

They piled into Baba's (very cool) car and Baba honked the horn as they drove off.

'Oh, and more good news,' he said. 'Your mum's arrived safely and is going to call you later.'

'**YEYYYYYY!**' Keita squealed.

'Cool,' Shara said. Then she suddenly

remembered and looked around the back seat.

'Hey, Keita, where are your Worries?'

'Oh, I left them with Abby,' he said. 'She said I could, just for the night. She said my Worries might be smaller once I've had a good night's sleep. She also showed me some ways to keep my Worries small.'

'Did someone say *worries*?' Baba said, turning on his radio.

'Yeah, but it's nothing,' Keita said. 'They've gone now.'

'That's the spirit!' said Baba, turning the music up. 'Here, listen to this tune! **DON'T WORRY . . . BE HAPPY!**' he sang along to the music. 'We're going to have a great couple of days together, you'll see!' He grinned in the car mirror.

When they got to Baba's flat, Keita and Shara immediately clambered on to the new bunkbeds Baba had bought especially for them.

'Hopefully this'll be the first
of *many* sleepovers!' he chuckled,
and Shara hoped so too.

After they'd had their extra-special
milkshakes and played board games with
Baba, Shara went and did her homework in
the spare bedroom. The room was still a bit
unfinished, but Baba had bought them special
bedcovers: **ALIEN PETSHOP**™ for Shara and
Dream Bunnies for Keita. Baba had even

got him pull-up pants, like the ones he had at home, just in case he had an accident in the night. At least that might make her brother feel less worried, Shara thought.

In the living room Keita was frowning at the words for his spelling test when Baba's phone rang. But Baba was cooking with the radio playing so he didn't hear it.

'It's **MUM!**' Keita yelled, looking at the caller display.

Baba came in but he was too late to answer the call.

'Oh **NO!**' Keita cried. 'We **MISSED** her!' He stared forlornly at the screen.

'It's no big deal!' Baba said.
'We'll just call her straight back.'
He tapped the phone and Mum's
face appeared on the screen like
magic.

'Hi, Mum!' Keita waved frantically.

'Hi, cutie-pie!' Mum grinned. 'Lovely to
see you!'

'Where **ARE** you?'

'I'm in my hotel! It's really swish – look!'
Mum turned the camera round to show
Keita: there was a big bed, a desk,
flowers, a bowl full of fruit, an
ENORMOUS TV ... 'The girls
and I are just about to play a

85

match and then go out for a meal.'

Keita was pleased to see Mum was having a nice time. But then he suddenly felt anxious. 'I've got a spelling test tomorrow!' he shouted at the screen.

'Oh! Well, make sure you –' The phone crackled and Mum froze.

'WHAT?' Keita shouted.

'MAKE SURE I WHAT?
I CAN'T HEAR YOU!
YOU'VE FROZEN!'

Just then Shara ran in. 'Is that Mum? Can I talk to her?'

'No, you can't, she's *frozen*!' Keita moaned,

pulling the phone closer to him.

'Just let me see her!' Shara said, trying to get the phone off him.

'**HEY!**' Keita yelped.

The phone suddenly came alive again with Baba's ringtone:

DOOWOP DOOWOP DOOWOP SHABIDA BINGYBONG!

'**MUM?!**' Keita shouted, as he answered the call.

Mum's face appeared again but this time she was all blurry.

'Hi, Mum!' Shara said, squeezing her face

into the screen (as much as Keita would allow her).

'Sorry, sweetie,' Mum said. 'The reception here is terrible. Can you see me OK?'

'Not really . . . and you sound very far away,' Shara said, trying really hard not to sound cross. Keita had got to see Mum properly. It was SO unfair.

'How was school?'

'Erm, OK . . . I – I –'

Shara hesitated, not wanting to tell

Mum about the Worries. But before she could, Keita interrupted anyway. He was so **ANNOYING!**

'**MUM!** I've got a spelling test tomorrow!' he yelled.

'I know, cutie-pie, I heard. You'll be fine. Just make sure –'

The phone crackled again. Mum's video cut out.

'Make sure **WHAT?!**' Keita yelled at the phone. '**OOOOH!** Lost connection. **AGAIN!**'

Baba came back in from the kitchen. 'How's your mum?' he said. 'Everything all right?'

'No, it's not all right.' Keita frowned,
crossing his arms and turning away.

'Well, at least YOU got to talk to her,'
Shara sulked. 'I only said ONE thing.'

'So did I!'

'Hey, hey,' said Baba. 'Let's calm
down, shall we? Look, dinner's ready now.
Maybe we can try to call Mum back after
you've got something **YUMMY** in your
TUMMIES, OK?'

Then Baba tickled Shara and Keita's
tummies like he used to do when they were
both really little, and they laughed, in spite
of all the trouble with the call. They sat
down at the dining table and ate Baba's

vegetable stew, special rice and homemade bread. They ate up every last bit, and even cleaned their plates with the bread. It was **DELICIOUS!** Shara was glad that Keita's Worries seemed to have disappeared so they could really enjoy their dinner.

In fact, Shara and Keita had a lovely evening with their Baba, despite all the Worries earlier in the day. After dinner, they played some more games and listened to Baba play the piano. They were having so much fun, they even completely forgot about calling Mum back.

Until Reece Sponsable popped his head up, that is . . .

Chapter 8

Shara had just put her pyjamas on and was looking for her and Keita's toothbrushes when Reece appeared from under her school clothes.

'Looking for *these*?' he said, thrusting two toothbrushes at Shara. He had already put their different

toothpastes on to the correct brushes.

'Oh. Hi, Reece.' Shara sighed. Relief mixed with dread seeped through her body. Relief, because Reece was so familiar, and he could actually be quite helpful – but then again, he was also **A HUGE PAIN IN THE BOTTOM**.

'You know you forgot to call your dearest darling mother back!' Reece tutted, following Shara to the bathroom.

Shara scrubbed her teeth and spat in the sink. 'We were *playing*. And having a nice time with Baba – we haven't seen him for ages! And anyway, the reception was bad.'

'Yes, but it might be better now. And you

haven't wished her goodnight. She's all alone in her hotel room, and she'll be wondering why you don't want to talk to her.'

Shara tried not to listen. She knew her mum was probably having a nice time with her friends. But what if she wasn't . . .? That was the trouble with Reece. He was always so persuasive!

'Oh, and call Keita to brush his teeth,' Reece added.

And so bossy. But he had a point.

'KEITA!' Shara called obediently. 'Come and brush your teeth!'

After ten more shouts from Shara, Keita finally came bounding into the bathroom.

Shara handed him his toothbrush.

'Cool, it's the dinosaur again!' Keita said on seeing Reece, who was now inspecting Shara's teeth to make sure they were properly clean. Keita reached out to touch the spikes on his tail.

'Don't even think about it,' Reece snapped, flicking Keita's finger away. 'That boy has NO manners.'

'Time for bed!' Baba called from the bedroom. He was fluffing up the pillows and plugging in their night lights. The room was starting to look almost as cosy as their own bedrooms.

Keita was relieved to see that Baba had left him a pair of pull-up pants on the bed. At least wetting the brand-new sheets would be one less thing to worry about. He quickly slipped them on under his pyjama bottoms when no one was looking.

The three of them snuggled together on the bottom bunk under his new quilt. Keita frowned. It was a bit scratchy – not like his lovely soft sheets at home. Shara saw him frowning and tried to give him a 'cheer-up' smile.

Then Baba spoke. 'Oh, before I forget, your mum left a voice message for you!' He pulled out his phone, and Keita and Shara gathered round eagerly.

'Hi, kids, Mum here. I just wanted to say bye as we were cut off earlier! I'm about to go out now so I'll catch you tomorrow. Good luck with your spelling test, Keita. What I was trying to say earlier was, make sure you get a good night's sleep. No late-night revising! OK, love you all lots, kiss kiss, night night, bye bye!'

When they had finished listening to the message, they heard a noise coming from Keita's suitcase. It sounded like his Worries, which was strange. Keita thought that he'd left them with Abby at school, and that Mum's message would make him feel LESS worried too. Oh dear, it was all so confusing!

NO, I'M BIGGER THAN YOU!

WELL, YOU'RE JUST A SLIMY PIECE OF SLIME!

No, I'm bigger than you!

WELL, YOU'RE JUST A GIANT CRYING BABY!

HEY, CUT IT OUT! YOU'RE BOTH GIANT BABIES!

'What on earth is that noise?' Baba said, staring at the suitcase. 'Is that one of your toys or something?'

Shara and Keita gave each other a knowing look. But neither of them said anything.

'Mmm-hmm.' Keita nodded. He definitely didn't want to let his Worries out of that suitcase, not right now. He wanted to get a good night's sleep before his test, just like Mum had said. He pulled out his bedtime books instead. 'Let's read a story!'

'Good idea!' Shara said, her eyes fixed on the suitcase, which was now starting to shake.

'OK!' said Baba. 'Now, which one would you like?'

When they'd got to the end of the story, Keita really wanted to sing his special Bedtime Boogie song, like he always did with Mum.

But he knew Baba didn't know it, so instead, he pretended to be asleep. He hoped that he might actually be able to fall asleep quicker that way . . . and he also hoped his Worries might go away then too. Like Abby at the Happy Place had said, if he got a good night's sleep, he might feel less worried.

After she'd said a last goodnight to Baba, Shara clambered up to the top bunk with her torch and started to read her book. It was one of the **ALIEN PETSHOP**™ books Jaz had given her. She was just at a really good bit – Slobba Snail was trying to invade Planet Mirth with the help of the Crazy-Eyed Caterpillar – when suddenly there was a *tap tap tap* on the book's front cover.

'Excuse me! But **WHAT** is this drivel?'

'Oh, Reece! Please leave me alone,' Shara moaned, peering over the top of her book. 'I just want to read my book in peace.'

'That's not a book, it's a comic. I've got proper books for you. **CLASSICS**.'

Reece slammed the **ALIEN PETSHOP**™ book shut and placed a different one in Shara's hands – one that smelled at **LEAST A HUNDRED** years old.

Shara wrinkled her nose – it did NOT look fun! 'I don't want to read this! It looks . . . really boring.'

'Don't be silly! I'll read it to you!'

'No, it's **FINE**, Reece, honestly –'

'I *insist.*'

Reece began to read in his softest voice, which unfortunately was still pretty shrill. The story was as boring as it had looked, and Shara was horrified to see that there were absolutely NO pictures. She sighed.

She'd known it was going to be rubbish just from the front. Who on earth said you can't judge a book by its cover, anyway? Surely that only applied to people.

Shara lay awake for what felt like **HOURS**, listening to Reece droning on, while she tossed and turned, put the pillow over her head, then took it off again, then back on again . . . until suddenly Keita appeared at the top of the ladder by the side of Shara's bed.

'I can't sleep!' he hissed.

'I can't sleep **EITHER!**' Shara whispered back.

'Can I sleep in your bunk?'

'No, there's not enough space.'

'PLEEEEEEEASE?'

But this wasn't actually a question, because Keita was already clambering in beside her. To Shara's surprise, he picked up Reece and tucked him under his arm, like a teddy bear.

'You go to sleep too, dinosaur,' he said, patting him on the head. 'Shh now.'

And to Shara's even greater surprise, Reece actually did.

In fact, they *all* did.

Chapter 9

The next morning everyone overslept, EVEN Reece. It was Scared who woke everyone up.

'HEEEEELP!' he shouted. 'HEEEEEELP! Someone help me DOWWWWN!'

Oh no! Shara thought. *Keita's Worries really*
are **BACK!**

She got up and went to where the noise
was coming from. She found Scared high up
on a shelf, trembling inside one of Baba's old
paint tins.

'How did you get up there?' Shara
gasped. 'I thought Keita had left you in

school, with Abby?'

'He did, but Badbye sneaked us out. And then they threw us up here cos we were making too much noise.'

'**BADBYE!**' Shara marched into the bedroom and picked Keita's Worry up. '**WHY** did you bring Keita's Worries home?'

'Because **I FELT LIKE IT**,' Badbye said, crossing their arms.

'You should have known this would happen, Shara,' Reece said, shaking his head. 'You've got to be firmer with Worries!'

'But *you're* a Worry!' Shara said, rolling her eyes.

'But *I* –' Reece said dramatically – 'am no *ordinary* Worry. I don't flap around. I get things **DONE**.'

'OK, well get this done: make sure Keita's ready for school before we're late!'

'FIIIINE,' he said, rolling his eyes.

'And round up the other Worries too. We can't leave them here. They'll probably break something.'

'I'll see what I can do,' Reece said confidently.

Shara quickly threw on her uniform and went to wake up Baba. But thankfully he was already in the kitchen, making – or trying to make – their packed lunches.

'I've put more rice and stew from last night's

dinner in little boxes
for you, OK? You can
heat it up at school.
And fruit for dessert.'

WARNING!
weird lunch
inside!!

yes, this
is an
actual
lunchbox

KEITA

'But we don't have microwaves at school,
Baba!' Shara said in a panic. She was already
imagining what her friends would say when
they saw her eating stew for lunch.

Just then Em appeared from behind the
kettle, making faces. She was mouthing
something to Shara: '*Sandwiches!*'

'The thing is, Baba,' Shara said awkwardly,
while making signs for Em to clear off.
'Usually, er, Mum just makes us sandwiches,
like everybody else.'

'Ah! Yes . . . I didn't think of that . . . '
Baba said. Shara was really hoping that
Baba would then pull out some bread and
cheese, but he just carried on spooning the
stew into the boxes. 'Well, you can eat it cold!'
said Baba brightly, seeing Shara's look. 'It'll still
be yummy.'

Shara grimaced. Em hopped up and
down on the window ledge and frantically

pointed at the fridge. But Shara decided to ignore her. 'OK, Baba! I'm sure it will be . . . *yummy*,' she said unconvincingly.

She sat down at the table and poured some cereal in a bowl – at least, she thought, he had bought their favourite, **CHOCO WIZZOS**. 'Keita, come on!' she yelled. 'We have to leave in a minute!'

'Oh, we've got *plenty* of time,' said Baba. '*Don't worry . . . be happy!*' he sang.

Right on cue, Reece Sponsable came marching into the kitchen, dragging Keita and the other Worries behind him. Reece was bigger than before and looking slightly frazzled.

'Woah! Hang on a minute! Who is this motley crew?' Baba asked, his sleepy eyes now very wide awake. 'Don't tell me **THESE** are toys?'

'Er, it's a long story,' Shara said. 'I'll explain in the car. Keita, eat this!' she said, stuffing an apple in his mouth. 'Baba, we HAVE to go!'

'But I'm not dressed yet, Shara!'

'It doesn't matter! Come on! We're going to be late!'

Baba downed his cup of tea, wiggled his feet into his shoes and grabbed his keys.

'I'm not going **ANYWHERE!**' Badbye shouted as Reece carried them out the door.

'And neither are **YOU** – you'll see!'

Shara buckled all the Worries tightly into their seat belt while Baba tapped the school address into the map on his phone.

'It's OK, I know the way!' Shara said. 'Let's just **GO!**'

'Don't worry!' Baba said. He was far too relaxed for Shara's liking. 'We're all set. I'm just . . . typing . . . one . . . more . . . word . . . oops . . . delete . . . Great, off we go!'

'We're going to be **SOOOO** late!' Reece murmured out of the corner of his mouth. 'Mr Chatterjee is going to be so cross!'

Em started bouncing up and down nervously. 'Shhhh, Reece, you're really **NOT** helping!' Shara hissed.

'Did you say we're gonna be late?!' cried Keita. 'But what about my TEST?!'

Sad started to cry. 'Oh, *tests*! They always make me feel so SAD – especially if we get any answers wrong!'

'No crying on the seats!' Reece snapped. 'This is vintage leather!'

'Oh yes, **I HATE TESTS TOO!**'

Scared trembled. They huddled together, seeming to find some comfort in each other's misery.

'Hey, can you loosen the seat belt?' Badbye said, rather sweetly. 'It's pressing on my belly.'

'Fine.' Shara sighed, pulling it slightly. But before she knew it, Badbye had slipped out of the seat belt, **bounced** on to the front seat and **leaped** on Baba's phone.

'HEY –
what are
you doing?'

Shara shouted.

'We're going **HOME!**' Badbye grinned, tapping the phone a few times before sliding along the dashboard.

Baba, who was completely absorbed in the traffic and following the map on his phone, took a sharp turn to his left.

'This is the wrong way!' Shara shouted.
'Badbye, you changed the map!'

'Hee-hee!' The Worry grinned
mischievously.

'Stop following the map, Baba! We need
to turn round!'

'Oh! Goodness, how did that happen?' he
mumbled, looking very confused.

Reece whipped out a fancy device from
his briefcase. 'Leave it to me! I've got a GPS!
You're taking orders from me now, Grandad.'
He jumped into the front seat and proceeded
to shout and sign directions.

Em Barrass-Ment and Shara slunk back
in her seat. It was bad enough to be in a

funny car that everyone was looking at – it had no roof. But having Reece in the front seat looking like a cross between a military leader and a four-armed traffic warden was too much.

When they finally got to school, the gate was SHUT. This had never happened before, in all of Shara's life – not even when she was in Reception and Keita had wiped his dirty nappy all over the car seat.

'NOOOOOO!' she cried.

'Sooo, what happens now?' Baba asked, tightening the belt of his dressing gown.

'We have to ring the bell,' Keita said, hanging his head in shame. The Worries groaned in unison.

'What's the big deal, kid?' Baba said.

'It's just **SO** embarrassing,' Shara said moodily. This was NOT how she'd wanted the day to start AT ALL!

Just then, the caretaker, Mrs Laska, came out. 'Hello, hello!' she said cheerily.

Shara launched into a flustered explanation, full of sorries, which were echoed by Em.

But Mrs Laska cut them short. 'No worries at all! Things happen, Shara!'

Shara, Keita and their Worries lingered at

the gate, not quite believing that they weren't being told off.

'Well, come in then!' Mrs Laska laughed. 'But no rushing! Nice and calm!'

Baba waved them off. 'Have a **GREAT DAY**, kiddos. And you, little creatures, behave yourselves! See you later!'

Mrs Laska

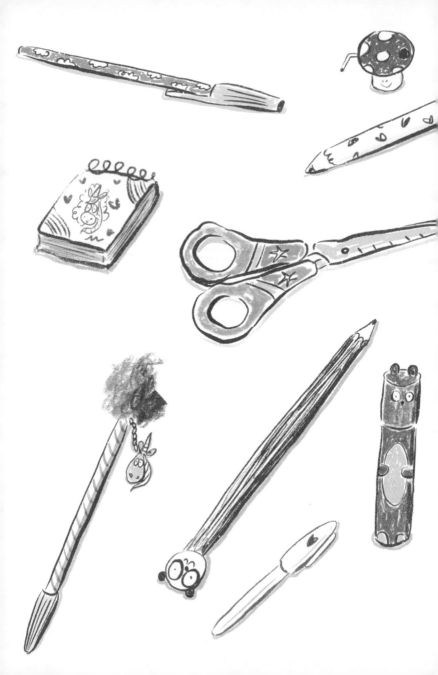

Chapter 10

When Shara got to class, she was so flustered she found it hard to concentrate on anything Mr Chatterjee was saying. Thankfully, Reece was writing things down for her.

Shara was beginning to feel really sleepy from the night before. She wondered what Mum was up to right now. Maybe she was

playing a netball game, or floating about in the pool . . . Shara felt her head go heavy and her eyes start to fall, like metal shop shutters. The next thing she knew, she was drifting into a deep sleep and dreaming the strangest of dreams.

Even Mrs Azizi, the teaching assistant,
was there. She was touching her arm, saying,
'Shara, Shara! Wake up! She's fast
asleep, poor thing.'

OH NO! That was what Mrs Azizi
was saying IN REAL LIFE! Shara
lifted her head and saw that everyone was
laughing. Em Barrass-Ment suddenly leaped
on to her desk, even bigger than before, and

tried to cool Shara's hot cheeks with a cold flannel. Shara batted her away and hid her face in her hands. Everyone laughed even harder.

'All right, calm down, class!' Mr Chatterjee said, above the noise. 'It's not kind to laugh at our classmates.'

Mrs Azizi gave Shara a reassuring smile. 'It's OK, don't worry, Shara.'

Shara wished everyone would **STOP** saying that. If she could stop worrying, then **OF COURSE** she would, but right now Reece was literally dancing on the desk and waving his arms at her frantically. Why, exactly, Shara wasn't sure. It was like he was trying to tell her something.

'If you're not feeling well, Shara, you can go to the school nurse, you know,' Mrs Azizi said kindly. 'Or maybe you'd like to chat with Abby?'

Shara would have liked a chat with Abby, but she was worried about all the work she would miss. Reece would be so cross.

'Say **NO!**' Em Barrass-Ment whispered in her ear. 'No, no WAY!'

'Er, no, I'm fine, thanks, Mrs Azizi,' Shara mumbled. 'I was just a bit sleepy, that's all. Sorry.'

Shara picked up her pencil and managed to stay awake until break time, when Em dragged her off. After falling asleep in class, they needed somewhere good to hide. Keita and the Worries searched everywhere but they couldn't find her.

After break, when she got back to class, Shara was pleased to discover they had a surprise test – at least that meant no one was looking at her and she didn't have to speak to anyone.

At lunchtime, of course, her friends had a **MILLION QUESTIONS**:

WHERE WERE YOU AT BREAK?

DID YOU GO TO THE NURSE?
DID YOU GO TO ABBY?

Did you get in trouble?

Were you on the toilet?
Did you fall asleep on the toilet?

Are you asleep right now?

WHAT'S THE MATTER WITH YOU!?

Shara could feel tears starting to sting her eyes. She never cried – never ever – so this felt WEIRD. Em gave her a hug and wouldn't let go. Shara lifted her head and swallowed the tears back. Then she opened her lunch box . . .

'MY LUNCH!' Shara cried. 'You've eaten it ALL!'

Reece Sponsable, Sad, Scared and Badbye pointed to a new Worry, whose mouth was stuffed full of rice.

'It was her!' they all said at once.

'Who are you?!' Shara said, slightly disgusted. This Worry looked nothing like Reece or Em. She was pretty . . . *greedy*.

Reece bustled forward. 'That's Missy Meltdown. She doesn't talk.' Reece lowered his voice. '*She just screams.*'

Missy Meltdown carried on stuffing the remaining **scraps** of Shara's lunch into her very wide mouth. When she'd finished, she let out a squawk, which Reece seemed to understand.

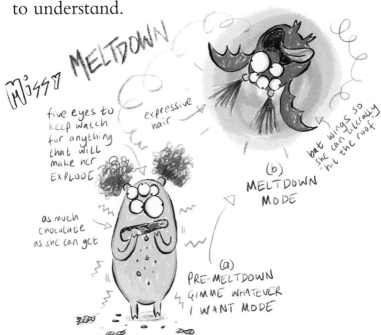

MISSY MELTDOWN

five eyes to keep watch for anything that will make her EXPLODE

expressive hair

bat wings so she can literally "hit the roof"

(b) MELTDOWN MODE

as much chocolate as she can get

(a) PRE-MELTDOWN GIMME WHATEVER I WANT MODE

'Here!' he said, pulling a pear out from his briefcase. Missy Meltdown squawked again, only louder.

'I'm not giving you chocolate, Missy. You can have fruit.'

Missy Meltdown stomped her foot and squawked **EVEN** louder. She seemed to be . . . changing colour . . . and shape!

'Just give her whatever she wants!' Scared wailed. The other Worries looked on with a mixture of horror and fascination. Missy Meltdown looked like she was going to . . .

EXPLODE!

Reece quickly threw her a chocolate bar, which she tore apart in seconds.

Suddenly Shara heard Keita's voice across the lunch hall. He was headed towards her, followed by a **big**, lumbering, furry creature.

'Shara! I've been looking for you EVERYWHERE!'

'What on **EARTH** –'

'My spelling test went TERRIBLY!' he wailed. 'Thanks to **LOSER** here.'

'That's not very nice, Keita.'

'No, that's actually his name. Loser. He's another Worry!'

Loser gave an awkward wave and mumbled, 'H'llo.'

never-brushed hair

one eye for only seeing what is bad

stinky fur

loved by flies

dirty feet

Loser

Keita continued breathlessly. 'He gave me a piece of old chewing gum instead of an eraser,  then he spilled Miss Dandelion's Tippex all over her desk and THEN he scrunched up my spelling test and . . . and . . . **ATE IT!**'

Keita was interrupted by more squawking noises. Missy Meltdown had finished several bars of chocolate by now, including ones from other kids' packed lunches, and she was badgering the other Worries for more.

'I've got nothing left!' Reece said, all four hands in the air, his briefcase emptier than it had ever been.

Missy Meltdown
grunted and shrieked
and began to . . .
sprout WINGS!?
She was turning
darker and louder by the
second and soon was rising to the ceiling.

'SHE'S GONE COMPLETELY WILD!'
Reece shouted as she circled the room like
a bat.

The whole lunch hall was watching now
while Em Barrass-Ment grew bigger and
bigger. Shara was absolutely mortified and
for the first time in a long time, she began to
actually . . . CRY!

Chapter

Shara's tears
came thick and fast.
Sad was particularly impressed.

Her friends came rallying
round to give her hugs and say
kind things. Even Chip Monk, a
big boy in her class, patted her
on the shoulder.

Keita, who was trying to
remember the last time he had
seen his sister cry, stood stock-
still as if his feet

were glued to the ground (it was actually just Scared, clinging on to his ankles).

Mrs Cherry, who was on lunch duty, appeared through the little crowd. 'Oh dear, Shara. What's wrong?' she asked in a soothing voice.

'I want . . .

I want . . .

my . . . mum!'

Shara sobbed quietly in Mrs Cherry's ear.

Mrs Cherry smiled sympathetically and took her to one side. 'Come on,' she said. 'Shall we go and see Abby?'

Shara nodded and already felt a bit calmer. She was looking forward to going somewhere quiet and telling someone about her Worries.

Shara felt **EVEN BETTER** once she was sitting down in that sunny room, talking to Abby. Shara had been worried about seeming silly for missing her mum when she'd only been gone for one night – especially at her age. But Abby was a really good listener and helped her realize that it wasn't silly at all. It was completely *normal*. As soon as Abby said that word, Em Barrass-Ment immediately shrank. Em was so happy, she spent the whole time curled up on Abby's lap like a sleepy (mousey) cat.

As they talked, Missy Meltdown came back down to the ground and tucked her wings back in. She even stopped squawking

and started to use actual words. Reece
Sponsable, who refused to listen to anything
at first and tried everything to leave the
room, eventually realized that the *responsible*
thing to do was to open his ears and . . .
listen. As soon as he did, he was much
calmer. Instead of running around, always
doing things, he sat **COMPLETELY STILL**.
Even *he* started to shrink.

At home time, Keita joined Shara in the
playground, his Worries still trailing behind
him. Shara was surprised to see that Reece
Sponsable, who was now small enough to fit
in her pocket, did not jump down to greet

them or fuss around them like he normally did.

'HI, KIDS!'

Baba called, waving. Shara was happy to see he was no longer in his dressing gown. She (and Em) gave him a big hug and took a deep breath – Shara loved how Baba's clothes always smelled of paint and lavender. It was so soothing.

'**Hi** . . .' Keita said sadly.

'**HEY!** What's up, little man?' Baba frowned. Then he spotted Keita's Worries. 'Woah, these guys have got bigger since this morning. Want to tell me all about it?'

He took him by the hand and Keita introduced Baba to all his Worries.

On the journey home, Baba listened and nodded and listened and nodded. When they got back to his flat, he said, 'I know exactly what we need to do with these Worries! Just give me one second!'

Baba started pulling out brushes and pots and blank canvases. Then he squeezed some paint into trays.

'RIGHT— COME ON, YOU LOT!'

he said, beckoning Shara, Keita and their Worries over. He gave them all aprons, even the Worries. 'Let's **PAINT!**'

At first Em Barrass–Ment
and Loser wouldn't let Shara
and Keita even so much as pick
up a paintbrush. Thankfully
Baba distracted them with some
fluorescent paint and soon they
were painting their own
surprisingly big pictures.
Baba encouraged
them all to be **FREE**
with their brushes and
even throw paint at the

canvas. 'Paint **ALL** your
feelings!' He laughed.
'Every last drop of them!
Don't be afraid to express yourselves!'
He even put some funky music on for
them to paint to.

  By the end they were all
splattered with paint
– and so was the living room.
But everybody was much
happier – especially the
Worries!

Chapter 12

The next day, Baba woke Shara and Keita up early with the smell of their favourite breakfast: pancakes! The Worries took a bit longer to wake up (they all wanted a lie-in after yesterday's excitement).

As they sat down to eat, they saw that Baba had hung their paintings up on the wall.

Shara looked at hers and all the colourful, funny lines wriggling around the canvas. It was very different from drawings she normally did, which were always so straight and neat. She felt proud. And strangely relieved.

'Fantastic paintings!' Baba exclaimed. 'How are we feeling today, kids?'

'GOOD!' Keita shouted. 'I had a REALLY funny dream about sliding down a rainbow! AND –' Keita hesitated for a moment. 'I didn't have any accidents!'

'That's great news, Keita!' Baba said happily. 'How about you, Shara?'

'I definitely feel better,' she said. 'I *think*.'

Shara was so used to worrying, she wasn't sure how she felt about **NOT** worrying. It felt a bit like wearing socks with sandals. It was definitely warmer – but it just felt slightly . . . *weird*.

'You know, Shara,' Baba said quietly. 'You are a *fantastic* big sister, but you are not responsible for Keita. He's got your mum and me looking out for him. That's for us grown-ups to do. You just carry on being a kid and having fun, **OK?**'

'**OK**.' Shara smiled. She felt relieved again. Yes, it really *did* feel like warm socks.

'Now,' said Baba. 'Talking of **FUN**, I want you to remember to paint or draw your cheeky Worries from now on. It doesn't have to be anything fancy. Just some **squiggles** will do.'

'Is that what you do, Baba?' Keita asked.

'As a matter of fact, it is!' Baba said, laughing. 'That's actually how I became an artist. Whenever I felt worried, I'd pick up a paintbrush and put my Worries into a painting.'

'And did it help?' Shara asked.

'Oh yes!' Baba laughed. '**A LOT**. And now it's my job! So, Worries can be a pain, but they can sometimes be very inspiring too.' Baba pointed to one of his own paintings on   the wall. 'You see, that painting there is called *Sadness*, just like your Worry, Keita! And I think it's one of my most beautiful paintings.'

Shara looked at the painting carefully. She hadn't looked at it properly before, even though she'd seen it many times. It *was* beautiful, she realized.

'I've got an idea!' Baba said, suddenly getting up. 'I'm going to give you both your very own sketchbooks, so you can draw your Worries whenever you want.'

He opened one of his art cupboards and pulled out two brand-new sketchbooks for them. 'You can even decorate the covers if you like.'

Baba gave them some SPECIAL paint pens so they could draw on the covers of their new sketchbooks. It was really relaxing!

Afterwards, they got dressed, because Baba said he wanted to take them out. They went to lots of lovely places and did lots of lovely things.

It finished in the best WAY ever – with seeing Mum!

Shara and Keita had been having

SO MUCH FUN, that they had almost

forgotten she was coming home that evening!

They had so much to tell her – and so did

their Worries!

'Wow,' Mum said, when the Worries finished introducing themselves. 'Well, it's good to meet you all.' She took Shara and Keita in her arms. 'But I'm sorry they've caused you two so much trouble.'

'It's OK,' Shara said. 'We know how to handle them now.'

'Yeah!' said Keita. 'Abby showed us ways to keep our Worries small, like talking about them or writing or singing or playing games with them –'

'Don't forget **PAINTING**, too!' Baba added.

'Oh, YEAH!' Keita said excitedly. 'Look at our paintings, Mum!'

Mum spun round and looked at the bright, energetic pictures on the wall. 'Wow!' she said.

'Those are **SO** wonderful! Abby and Baba are right. It *is* super-important to express your Worries. It's much better to have that worrying fizzing around in those paintings than cooped up in your heads!'

'Hey, Mum,' Shara said hesitantly. 'Can we . . . stay another night?'

'Yeah! Can we, **PLEASE?!**' Keita begged.

'I thought you two would be desperate to get home!' Mum said, chuckling.

'So did I!' Keita said. 'But we've just been having so much fun!'

'You could stay too, Mum!' Shara said hopefully.

'Yeah, and then it would be a **REALLY BIG SLEEPOVER!!**' Keita yelled.

'PLEEEEEASE!' they said in unison.

'OK, OK!' Mum agreed. 'We'll all stay then!
I wanted to celebrate with you anyway. I scored
a goal for our team in the final netball match!'

'WOOHOOOO!'

Shara and Keita
shouted. 'Way
to go, Mum!'

'That's
brilliant!' Baba
cried. 'I think
that definitely calls for . . .

A PIZZA
CELEBRATION!'

yeah!

YEAH!

YEAH!

The next day, Baba's flat was unusually
quiet. Shara woke up Keita.

'Keita! Keita! Where are they?' she
whispered.

'Who?' Keita said, bleary-eyed.

'The Worries! They're not under the bed!'

'How should I know?'

Shara looked all around the bedroom
and in the cupboards. But there was no sign
of them there. She and Keita went into the
kitchen, the bathroom and the living room.
But there was no sign of them there either.

'You can't see them!?' Baba said, as he
poured some coffee into his mug. 'I guess that's
a good sign!'

'Why – can you, Baba?' Shara asked.

'Of course I can!' he said, laughing and staring
at the wall behind them. 'Look a bit harder!'

It was Keita who spotted them in the end.

'THERE! In our PAINTINGS!' he yelled.

He waved at them excitedly.
'Hiiiii!'

Sure enough, there were Sad, Scared, Badbye, Loser, Reece Sponsable, Missy Meltdown and

Em Barrass-Ment, in ridiculous poses in the paintings. But they were **FROZEN STILL**.

'I don't think they can hear you, Keita!' Baba said, chuckling.

As soon as he said it, Shara and Keita saw something: it was Reece, waving! It was just for a second. But it was enough for them to know that the Worries *could* hear them.

Keita and Shara smiled at each other, the way only brothers and sisters or great friends can. Their Worries had gone for now. One day, they might come back. But next time, Shara and Keita wouldn't feel so alone.

They would

ALWAYS

have each

other.